THE SINLESS FLOWER

Black Dust Collections
Volume 1

The Sinless Flower

T.K. Sai

Charleston, SC
www.PalmettoPublishing.com

The Sinless Flower

Copyright © 2023 by T.K. Sai

All rights reserved

First Edition

Hardback ISBN: 979-8-8229-0478-1
Paperback ISBN: 979-8-8229-0479-8
eBook ISBN: 979-8-8229-0480-4

Contents

THE FIRST YEARS

I would like to captivate you with a story of a young girl whom I once knew. This is definitely not a tale of rainbows and smiles but one of deception and transformation. This may not be a book that happy-go-lucky people would want to read, but if you enjoy a good mystery and betrayal story, this is for you.

A girl with impeccable etiquette lived in a magnificent place called Whistleleaf in Nes State, where a life of luxury was every resident's fate. She had parents who adored her and showed her love. Lirah possessed material wonders, all of the above. Just outside the entry of the town, an extravagant sign with bold, gold letters read, "Welcome to Whistleleaf Community: join the perfect life no one ever leaves." Everyone thought of Lirah as a sweet nine-year-old girl. She was exceedingly lucky for what she had. Was it not the life we all dream of?

Let us first go back a few years to the beginning with John and Violah. After wedding bells rang, five long years of visits to doctors and specialists failed mis-

erably. At first, their optimism ran high, but it soon vanished, because they believed that a healthy woman should not have had such an issue. Violah blamed God, as though it were another punishment from him. Quite ironic that she would mentally confess that God did not exist. According to her, bad things should never happen to good people, a belief based on her own standards, not God's.

One Friday after dinner, John brought Violah a gift, as he had always loved to shower her with the wonders of the world. It was unique, one to tame her heart and mind. He sat beside her. "I have something for you." "Oh, what is it?" she asked him. "Here, open it," he said. He gently pushed the rectangular present wrapped in silk cloth towards her. She looked at it, then him. "Is this what I think it is?" She unfolded the cloth, sighed, and said, "You very well know I have no interest in this." "This is not a..." he said. "I have no interest in this or anything like it." She was a firm believer in reality and science, upon which her mentality was predicated. "Please just try. You never know." He tried to convince her with his charming eyebrow raise. She nonchalantly agreed to read one page. "That is all I ask. One thing, try to feel the book, not just read it." She began to read; the more she read, the more intrigued she became. "Honey, listen to this," she requested.

Λ

"How many times have you heard that money is the root of all evil, but is it really? Money is an object; how can something contrived by mankind control humanity? Are we not in control of our minds, our lives? Regardless of its form, the desire and the drive to obtain it have, as records have shown, increased at an abysmal level. Many are acquiescent and would do almost anything to have it, including shameful acts or losing one's dignity, even to the point of literally selling one's soul. It is not necessarily money that individuals aspire to but the results it bestows. Especially within a capitalist society, the greater the surfeit of materialism one possesses, the higher the status one attains. Maybe the birth of money was how greed was born. Greed not only destroys the person possessing its sin but those in its path and does not cease its proclivity. Greed has polluted our planet; though the state of the world is obvious, many people choose to remain in the same lifestyle. Many denote having objects as wealth and put such value on retaining their riches above others. There are some who have woken up, but before we all do, will it be too late? If we have God, basic necessities would suffice. There is nothing wrong with desiring objects; it is the excessiveness and the pain inflicted on others to have or keep the objects that is the problem."

As quickly as she became enthralled by the literature, she just as quickly grunted once she saw a particular line. No one knew why bitterness filled her heart, not even her love. She slammed the book down and went to take a bath. John returned to the kitchen from gardening in the backyard and saw the book upside down. "I guess she did not like it," he mumbled. It lay facedown on one of its folded, crinkled pages. John shook his head and looked up with his bottom lip folded in and pushed up towards his top lip and decided to just let it go. Anytime he brought up the topic, she completely dismissed him until it eventually became a thing of the past. Herein lies the internal question: Should he choose his wife or his faith?

After a long day of work, John met solitude as he walked through the door. Violah was out as usual, somewhere unbeknownst to him. Her secret passion, which had been prevalent for the past three years, remained the center of her life. John walked through the house. *Where is she?* He took his shoes and dark coat off and placed them in the closet. His eyes darted back and forth. He slowly walked down the stairs, his shoulders bouncing as he took each step. He decided to jump rope, a pastime he had rarely taken up since marriage. Grasping his rope, again and again he swung it over his head until droplets from his face hit the floor.

The whistling increased as he swung faster and realized three minutes had become difficult over the past twenty years. John rubbed his shins. "It has been a while," he proclaimed. "Why do we not have a child? John is a good person who pays his bills, with no criminal record. I help people and make donations." He spoke boldly. "Why do you never say anything? Talking to the wind would be more successful. At least I can feel it." He failed to understand that his notion of a good person was irrelevant; it is the relationship that matters. Not uttering a word in years to someone and then expecting communication would make no sense, but somehow this is expected of God.

Violah came home famished and went to satisfy her craving for pancakes. John heard the refrigerator close. His index finger and thumb firmly pinched the bridge of his nose. He took a few seconds to stare at the inside of his eyelids. Consequently, he decided to keep his feelings at bay with a blissful demeanor. He slowly walked upstairs mentally preparing himself. "How was your day?" "It was good," she replied. "Where have you been?" he asked. She chuckled and refused to answer. He tried to play it off with a slight smile. "Honey, would you make dinner tonight?" he asked her. "You know I do not do that, because I am not my mother," she told him. "Yeah, I loved that my mother cooked for my father, and

you know, I like cooking for you, but it would be good if you would cook for me sometimes, because I work twice as many days. It would be great to come home to a hot meal. I mean, you are at home more, especially for the last almost two years." He let out his feelings as he held her hand and stared at her. She crossed her arms and hummed. "Do not bother me. I must practice for the symphony!" she said as she walked past him to go prepare for bed. He looked down at intricate patterns of the tiles. "I see," he said as he left her be. He scratched his head and let out a long sigh. "Another day, another meal alone." He sensed a prelude to a failed relationship. He knew, yet chose to remain in denial and not confront her about her transgressions. He provided such luxury yet could not understand her unhappiness. John was not the type to quit or give up on anything. Maybe his reason for staying was due to his subtle faith. Once a devout man, over time he had lost his spunk and eagerness to pursue faith. It was sucked away, leaving only a minuscule remnant, just like their once-intimate relationship.

CHAPTER 2

A SURPRISE

John and Violah's career marked them a wealthy family. Violah's consummate instrumental talent established her as a locally renowned violinist. Her ambitious nature, which spanned over a decade, stemmed from her desire to prove that no higher power was necessary in her life. On the other hand, John was a simple, introverted artistic man who loved standing in front of the stove, cooking for his wife. His meals were the best in town; people from all over visited his establishment, Delectable, to partake in the tasting of scrumptious dishes. They lived in the most affluent county in Nes State. Many in their neighborhood loved passing their residence for even the shortest glance at its spectacular architecture. The hill it sat atop facilitated an amazing view overlooking a crimson-red lake. Though they lived like the 1 percent, aspects of Violah's life seemed to be governed by her lamenting. The past, more often than not, had a way of rearing its ugly head. After those five long years of disappointment, years dedicated to their

crafts pushed their deepest yearnings aside. They continued on, living their lives day by day.

Fast forward a few months to a foggy Sunday morning. Violah woke earlier than usual. She turned on the news. John walked in the room. "Oh my dear me, did you see the news?" she asked. "I just woke up, did not see anything yet," he answered with his eyes halfway open. "Absolutely ridiculous! Sixty-three people killed and injured by some loser with a gun!" she shouted. Why does this keep happening? All these things going on, and crime is rising. Murders, stealing, children being hurt. I mean, this is just like those riots that have been going on for the past few years over that guy who was murdered, supposedly their new leader. How much longer does this need to happen before people change?" she said as John listened and rubbed his forehead. "I need to go for a run because being in the world today makes me sick," Violah said. She threw on her sneakers and stormed out the door. She jogged, every few minutes glancing at her watch to see if she was making good time. After three miles, she came to a large hill, a challenge she had yet to master. "This time I will make it to the top!" she yelled out. She took a deep breath and charged up the hill. About halfway, she touched her lower abdomen as movement became a strenuous effort. She struggled home like a closed wallet. Mr. Grey

dashed to her, catching her head before it hit the corner of his step. Pitch black surrounded her. Sirens could be heard all over, wailing from the bumpy ride. Images went in and out. John's voice soothed her troubled mind, and then complete darkness came upon her. She blinked a few times as bright overhead lights awoke her. "Good evening, I am Dr. Tyme. How are you feeling?" "I feel fine," Violah replied. "I am so happy that you are okay!" John said. All he could do was smile at her. "What is going on?" Violah asked. "Something terrific for the two of you, I presume," Dr. Tyme said. John gripped her hand, covering it like a glove. "How did this happen?" Violah asked. "Just count your blessings, and worry about details later. I will leave you two to celebrate," said the physician. John pulled her face close to his. "We did it, Honey." Of course, they attributed nothing but her barren womb to God's will.

For the next few months, she stayed bedridden, relaxing and stuffing her face with all her cravings. As she rocked in her favorite chair, the incessant creaky noise became music to her ears. She sewed tiny clothes each day to add to a wardrobe pile that she laid on the table, as classical music played invariably. Allowing it all to soak in, she rested her head back, and little butterflies, fruit, and birds dangled in a circle above. After a while she became bored and decided to turn on

the television. "Great, more crime! Does it ever end?" she mumbled, throwing up her hands. John's truck rumbled, and she quickly turned it off. He opened the door and ran inside, ready to pounce on her. She yelped, "What are you doing?" "Having fun. I have not been this happy in years!" Her pearly whites sparkled. "I love you and am truly sorry." She did not know just how lucky she was. "I know, but none of that matters now, because I have forgiven you a while ago," John said and then kissed her forehead. He noticed her disappointment. "What is wrong, and why are you watching the news again, because you know it makes you upset?" he asked. "I want to stay informed. Look at this mess. You cannot say anything without making someone upset, even if it is reality. No one wants to be on the opposing side, and they are the most hypocritical scum on earth." He rubbed her shoulder, then went to shower. Bubbles from his new, lavender-mint soap ran down his back. His happiness brought him to sing, something he would never do. John rubbed the towel over his wet body. He dressed himself in new trousers along with a button-up collared shirt. John walked into the living room, and Violah was not there. He walked closer from behind the couch. There she lay, facedown and belly pressed on the carpet. "I will call the ambulance! Hold on!" Being in the waiting room

drained his patience. His focus was compelled by floral paintings of eccentric women standing with reins in their hands. A red handprint indented his cheek, and his eyes swelled after an hour of being shut. "You can see your wife now, Mr. Imra," the nurse said. He slowly made his way through the double doors and stopped when he noticed her room number was 777. "God, are you trying to tell me something?" he asked. He entered to find her holding a bundle of yellow blanket. That unassuming, adorable face struck him at once. "Thank you," he whispered. "Who are you talking to?" she asked as she noticed him looking up. "I am just thankful that you and our baby are healthy and safe," he told her. "Everything is perfect. What shall we name her?" Violah asked. "I told myself years ago that if I ever had this opportunity, I would give my child my mother's name," he said. "I think that is a wonderful idea," she agreed.

CONNIVING

Nine years later, one early morning on Airborn Way, a girl lay peacefully beneath her thick cotton blankets; green curtains laced with purple ribbon hung from her grand windows. Every toy a child's heart could desire sat upon her colossal shelves. The sun peeked through Lirah's curtains, washing over her face with gentle, warm rays, and a savory aroma permeated throughout her room. Curiosity rushed her downstairs, where her mother was making breakfast and lunch for her father. Her little face gravitated over a large, simmering pot of red soup. "Hmm, the food smells delicious. What are you cooking?" "Patience, wait and see." "Oh, how long?" Lirah whined. "Breakfast will be finished later than usual, not until nine o'clock." "My stomach feels so empty." "A smoothie will tide you over." "Oh, yeah! I guess. I love smoothies!" Her mother poured dates, apricots, and peaches into the blender. The whirling fruit locked Lirah's eyes until her mother pushed the off button. She gulped down a cup, noticing it made her full to the brim.

She sat with her eyes glued to the TV. Violah thought the music was interesting, until certain lyrics played. "Ah, what are you watching?" Violah asked. To her surprise, her daughter was viewing a moral atrocity, some self-proclaimed singer for children with atrocious talent, performing an inappropriate dance on the lap of the leader of the Underworld. Violah ran over to turn off the TV so quickly she almost tripped. "Mom, is everything okay?" Lirah asked. "Please, just go play," Violah said. "Okay, I will," she said as she scrunched up her face. "May I go to the park?" she asked with fingers clasped. "Sure, not too far," Violah answered. She could see the park's playhouse from the kitchen window. Lirah always enjoyed playing in the playhouse, which was similar to a cottage, with one window on each of its four sides. It was furnished and decorated like a house; it even had lights and bells overhead that chimed with each entry and exit. In fact, visiting the playhouse was the pastime of all the children in the town. Lirah recognized a few girls from school through the playhouse window. She entered. "Do you want to play with us?" the children asked. "What are we going to play?" Meelo asked Sam. "We should play Tree Catcher," Lirah interjected. "What is that?" Sam asked. "We are going to run, and whoever is it will try to catch everyone. If you touch the tree, you are safe, but if the person who is

it touches you, then you stop." "That is easy. We can do that," said Sam. "Meelo is it!" Lirah said. Meelo ran after Sam, then Ahmi, and Lirah headed for the tree. Lirah reached for the tree, and just before she made contact, Meelo caught her. Lirah was filled with rage but masked it with a smile. Meelo jumped for joy. "Now it is my turn," Lirah said. "New rule. Everyone has to climb up the tree to be safe." "This game is more funner than I thought! I guess you are not so bad after all," said Ahmi. "Ready, everyone? Go!" said Lirah. Lirah chased the girls and caught Ahmi and purposely allowed Meelo to climb up the tree. "OK, switch! New game, hide and seek!" Sam asked, "You can switch like that?" "It is my game," Lirah replied. Sam, Ahmi, and Lirah went hiding as Meelo counted to ten. As she counted, "Five... six...seven..." she stood up to prepare to jump down. Lirah furtively went behind the tree and pushed Meelo, sending her careening to the ground, knocking out two of her teeth. Her dress became drenched as her mouth and chin dripped with blood. Screams brought Ahmi and Sam out of hiding as Lirah stood in front of them. She held her teeth when Lirah stretched out her hand. "I never lose." She skipped away with the two tiny prizes in her pocket.

She arrived home to her parents conversing with her grandparents. Her foot tapped like a rabbit. She thought the phone call would never end. "Love you, bye, Mom and Dad," Violah said, and she placed the phone back on the wall, *click*. "Mom, for my birthday, may I have a new dress and a purple cake shaped like an L, like my name? I also want this," she added, showing her mother a unique, magical flower featured in *Worldly Magazine*, Violah's favorite subscription. She read that it could only be found in one museum in a small town on the continent of South Elo. With her back to Lirah, she sliced more potatoes, forcing the knife through so hard that indents set into the cutting board. "We will think about it. Besides, we should make a list for your party. It is not too far away."

John kissed Lirah and headed towards the front door. "Hey, wait, I saw her watching something that made me concerned. I will just say the guy was dressed unnaturally," she told him. "I told you so many times to get rid of that idiot box, but you still want it. It is just a bunch of filth, and nothing good comes from it." "Fine, it will be gone before you return. Always ruining my fun," she said as she made a pouty lip. Violah instructed Lirah to make certain her room was tidy. "I need to go to work. I do not have time for this right now," he said and kissed Violah, then left. "When you are finished, we will play that game you wanted to play," her mother said. "Actually, I want to draw, because I have been

practicing, and I am really good now." She gleamed at her while she tilted her head. Violah had always seen her as someone who could do no wrong. She went to her bedroom, closed her dark curtains, and then lay down. A few hours later, ringing woke her. The clock read a little after four; she slept longer than anticipated. She walked into the living room. "Honey, when will you be home?" She hung up the phone. The house was quiet. Violah walked up the stairs and cracked the door open. Lirah was writing in a book unrecognizable to her. Violah gently closed the door, and then knocked. "You can come in." The book was out of sight, so she did not mention it. Violah wondered why she hid it; never before had she hidden anything from her parents, or at least Violah had no knowledge of anything she hid. *Dun dun dunnnn...* She shrugged and went back downstairs to make dinner.

John came home to a family always delighted to see him. "I love coming home because it always smells so good in here. Is dinner ready?" "Hmm, do you really need to ask?" she said with arms folded. "I love that you cook so well! I will go get cleaned up and be back in about ten minutes." He bumped her with his hip as he walked by her. Lirah began salivating next to the savory noodles. "Do not eat; we must wait for your father." "Mom, but I am hungry now!" Lirah said. "Fine,

go ahead, take a few bites." John sat down, and they began to eat. Lirah picked at her food. "What is wrong? Why are you not eating?" John asked. "What is Jesus?" "I think you mean who is Jesus," John corrected her. Violah suggested that they should focus on eating. "Where did you hear that?" John asked. "Does it matter?" Violah interjected. John told her she should calm down and that it was simply a curious question. "We should just eat," Violah insisted. She stared, and John kept his head down towards his plate for the remainder of the meal.

CHAPTER 4

THE RAIN

Whistleleaf Elementary School was a brilliant structure, embellished from ground to roof with planters of tulips of every color, where formative minds spent four days a week, six months a year consuming food for their brains. Every adult in the school thought Lirah to be nothing less than a bright and respectful child. She was bright indeed, enough to fool the adults in town. You see, she was immensely intelligent for her age, but not even her parents conceived of her true potential. Lirah was quite likable to most and possessed the aforementioned attributes, yet her life was but a facade.

The students sat before their history teacher. "I am going to tell you a story instead," the teacher said. They were thrilled to hear there would be no school-work or homework. She began telling them how societies were when she was a child. She explained how she was taught to treat people with decency based on their character and deeds, not the brand someone wore, where they shopped, or what kind of phone

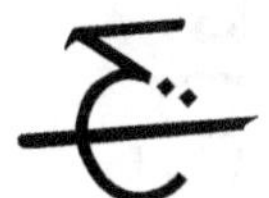

they purchased, which was also because there were no phones at that time. "The way the world turned into a trash zone full of people who censor every part of others' lives is unbelievable," she said to the class. She proceeded to tell them that if people in her day were to pathologize the behavior that people had in her old age, the world would have ended years ago. "Most people are so worried about not hurting others' feelings that they hide the truth so that they can be polite." Mrs. Keefworth tried to get them to understand as they held their mouths open with glazed eyes. "One day you will understand. It is time to go to your next class. Think about what I told you," she said. They trampled on to their math class. Ahmi wanted to ask Mrs. Keefworth a question but failed to find the words and left. "Who is ready to learn today?" Mr. Keefworth asked. He began to ask multiplication questions. Lirah answered all of them, and the rest of the room remained silent. "What do we always say?" the teacher asked. "Learning is good / We need to count and read / We understood / We need to lead / Education is key / From it, we will not flee," they responded in unison. "That is correct; therefore, everyone should at least try to participate," he said. A boy's voice from behind blurted out, "Give us a chance!" Lirah replied, "You are not quick enough." The teacher suddenly

had an idea to play Speed Product, which would give everyone a chance to answer. "Only answer when I call you. Eight times three...four times nine...twelve times three...Lirah, do you know twelve times twelve?" "The answer is 144." "Correct!" he said as he smacked the table. *Of course*, she thought. She glared, then smiled at the boy, though seething inside. He quickly brought his gaze to the world map on the wall and fidgeted with his pencil. The classmates scurried at the sound of the bell. He remained by the window. "Phew, safe," he said to himself as he grabbed his bag and walked outside to head home. While light rain tapped his T-Rex hat, he walked to his house a few blocks down the road and played with his action figure. A five-dollar bill on the ground lay in front of his next step. "Cool! I am rich!" Suddenly, excruciating, sharp pain shot through his Achilles tendon, and he fell on the action figure. It impaled his face. Streams from his eyes and red flowed down the street with the rain. Behind thick bushes and in between leaves, eyes peered back at him, and the realization of who was there caused him more pain than what had transpired. He succumbed to terror, suffered a heart attack, and attempted to grab his chest. He could hear feet shuffling away through the leaves, through the yard's tall trees between the houses. Then, his right eye slowly closed.

Back from school, up the stairs Lirah stepped onto the creaky boards of the front porch. The vehicles' absence gave her an unsettling feeling. She gripped the doorknob and cautiously turned it. She went through the hallway into the kitchen. "No one is here. Where is everyone?" The kitchen was spotless. She turned and saw the table set with a beautiful dinner—her favorite dishes lay on the table: beets, pecan bread, steamed rice and vegetables, and smoothies. She wondered what the occasion could be. Her eyes twinkled. "Surprise! What do you think?" her mother asked as her parents popped out of the closet. Lirah jumped. "Ah! What is this, Mom?" They handed her a silver, embroidered envelope that read, "To our wonderful daughter, happy birthday." Clapping echoed off the walls as her desire to see what the envelope revealed heightened. "What are these?" "We have agreed the three of us will travel to South Elo." Violah informed her that their flight would depart the next day at 3:00 p.m., and she had already pulled her out of school for several days. "I am so happy!"

CHAPTER 5

STRANGE FLIGHT

The next day, the Imra family sat in the kitchen, the same as any other morning, familiar and tranquil. Violah sipped from her yellow mug, allowing the steam to warm her face while sniffing a heavenly aroma of ginger and peach. An abrupt knock at the door made her spoonful of soup pour down her shirt. She used her handkerchief to wipe herself off. Then, she put on a shawl and peeked through the window's violet stained glass. John stood beside her. "It saddens me to bring unfortunate news, but a terrible accident took the Thomas family's lives." They continued conversing for a few more moments, and then he closed the door behind the man. Devastated by the calamity, Violah contemplated a way to tell her daughter. She pondered the reason for the doleful expression on her mother's face. She knelt to her eye level. "Your aunt and uncle were found in their house, and little Jimmy on the sidewalk." Lirah expressed how much Jimmy would be missed as her head lay helplessly on her mother's shoulder. They solaced one another with arms wrapped tightly around

each other, and she smiled contently, as if no sadness were upon her. How conniving!

During the officer's visit, he informed John and Violah of a service that would be held in the park at one o'clock in honor of the Thomas family. Dressed in proper attire, they headed to the service. Brick-and-stone residential properties and manicured lawns made Whistleaf a sight to be sought. Stratus clouds grayed the scene. "Looks like rain," John said. The three of them kept to the sidewalk along marigold flower beds as Lirah held up her arms like a plane soaring through clouds over mountains, as she, in an attempt to balance herself on the curb, walked slowly, one foot in front of the other. Passing each house, she saw groups of seemingly amicable people in the backyard of Mr. Grey's home, gathered around a pool. Ethereal sounds of various instruments and singing traveled to her curious ears. Lines of people went under one by one. Somehow aware that one man's tears were jovial, her fascination grew as he was dunked. He rose to the surface while the hidden rays emanating from the sun shone upon his face, as though heaven had opened. "I love you, God, thank you so much for being in my life. I worship you!" he proclaimed in a dulcet voice. Violah realized Lirah was not beside her. They turned around and saw her observing the event as if her day had ameliorated. John waved her

over. She walked towards them and asked, "Are they try-ing to drown that man?" "That is called baptizing," John answered. He then saw a colleague up ahead and told Violah and Lirah he would catch up with them in a few minutes. The first thing that popped into Violah's mind were vitriolic thoughts towards the ordeal. "Well, Mom, what is baptizing?" "It is how people prove their belief in God," she answered. "Mom, why do they do that? What...what is God? Why do we not believe in God?" Violah ignored her questions. "Is that the same thing as praying? May we do baptizing?" "No, we do not have time, and it is simply silly religious stuff. Only ignorant people get caught up in that sort of thing," she said. "I want to try!" she insisted. "I said no, and I mean enough about it!" her mother scolded. Lirah's eyes widened, and her mouth opened. She went on about how much she disapproved of her curiosity about God. She finally sim-mered down and apologized for her acrimonious behav-ior. "I just do not want to talk about that anymore," she said. Lirah thought the matter would be mitigated if she just put her head down. "Thank you," Violah replied. Violah deemed her day utterly adulterated. She became easily apathetic towards the topic, as rationality and ma-terial wealth were the epitome of her ideal life. As they walked on, Lirah wondered what could possibly bring forth tears from a grown man. He possessed the most

ineffable smile. She yearned for that sort of joy, because most of her life had been spent in misery deep inside, as if something were absent from her heart. Unfortunately, the euphoria vanished once she stepped foot onto the park grounds.

Practically all of the chairs were taken. Heartache was rampant—an unfamiliar, unfathomable feeling among Whistleleafeans. A few classmates entered the playhouse, and she followed them inside. The children stood and backed away. "Where is Meelo?" Lirah asked. "Recovering," Ahmi answered. "Should have been more careful," Lirah remarked. They stated they knew she pushed Meelo and ascertained she was the cause of Jimmy's death. She leaned forward to make direct eye contact. "Accidents happen. You never know who will be next." A teacher from afar announced the eulogy would soon begin. Lirah forcefully knocked down the porcelain tea set and stole an apple-decorated napkin from it. "We will clean it up later, let's go!" said Sam. The children exited, but indignant Ahmi stayed behind to pick up the pieces of the teapot. She grumbled under her breath, rolling her dark brown eyes. Then, something hit the wall that lured her towards the sound. She poked her head outside; the window immediately came down strong. Her body twitched as crackling noises came from her

throat. Curiosity got the better of her. Dozens of tiny apples lay before her. Lirah skipped towards her mother. "Where were you?" she asked. Before she could even open her mouth, her math teacher called out, "Mr. and Mrs. Imra!" He walked over to express his condolences. "It was well known what a tight-knit family all of you were. I pray that your household will be able to move on." "Thank you," they replied. "Though I must say it is quite bizarre that they were all...you know...within minutes of one another. I know that it was an accident for Cara and Jim, but little Jimmy? It really shakes me to my core that something could happen like this, especially in our town. If I may ask, when was the last time you spoke to your sister before the incident?" John noticed Violah's altered demeanor. "We really need to go," John said. "Sorry. I should have kept quiet," the math teacher said.

They rushed to Windborn Airport as the time quickly approached. John thought they would not make it, yet they did with a few minutes to spare. Their skirts flowed behind them while their shoes clicked on the ceramic tiles. They handed over their tickets and boarded. Cool air hit Violah's face like a spring breeze as she gazed at the elaborate design, royal blue seats, bright red carpet, and purple crystal chandeliers. They sat, and she touched her cheek with her index finger and thought,

Amazing. The plane's engines began to roar. Meanwhile, Violah's breathing became more vigorous. "Honey, everything will be fine," John said. She clenched the seat, closed her eyes, and remembered an event from her childhood. The sky was gray, the wind blew, and sounds of thunder echoed in the atmosphere. A car pulled into the airport parking lot, section A. The innumerable vehicles made it difficult to find parking. After circling a couple of times, "There is a spot!" Captain Romi said. A stranger swerved, then stuck up a particular finger. "Better luck next time," the stranger yelled, along with a few choice words. Captain Romi said, "I swear, people today, it is indicative of the times." Little Violah asked, "Why do people say bad words? That is so mean, and he took your spot. He knew we wanted that spot." "You are a kind, innocent little girl," her mother said. "Honey, you see, some people do not care how they treat others. This is why it is so important to believe in God. That is where our morals come from. If you believe in God, you will follow his commandments," her dad explained. "I understand." "Well, I need to go now. I do not want to be late. Bye, sweetheart, I will see you soon," he said. "It is my birthday," said the child. "Happy birthday again. Remember, we agreed to celebrate when I get back. You are a big girl, eight years old," he told her. He suggested they should say a prayer. "Because God will keep

you safe," she said. They bowed their heads and began to pray. "Dear Heavenly Father, we thank you for all things: our family, our lives, and our blessings. Please let me have a safe flight and return home to my family. We worship you and praise you above all. In your mighty name, amen." "Please keep Daddy safe, please, thank you, God." Violah chimed in. He squeezed her tight and kissed her on the forehead, and then he went inside. Violah's eyes followed. She requested to stay until the plane took off and was out of sight. Her mother agreed. After approximately twenty minutes of gnawing her nails and her left palm plastered on the window, she asked, "Where is he?" There they remained in the vehicle, until finally the plane emerged from the clouds. They hopped out of the vehicle. The plane began to rapidly nose-dive. The heart of her mother dropped and so did her stomach as her fingertips dragged down her face. Screams could be heard across the parking lot; a tumult of shrieks from onlookers increased! Her mother gripped her shirt tight. "Daddy! God, you were supposed to keep Daddy safe. Why?" Little Violah balled up her fists as saliva flew through her teeth from strong exhales. Little Violah stood, feet glued to the asphalt, with a ghostly pale face.

Violah eventually relaxed her mind. She placed her arms on the armrests and planted her feet firmly

on the floor. Violin playing in her ears assisted with her situation. A couple of hours elapsed, and the three of them fell into a deep slumber. A bump by someone going down the aisle woke Lirah. She scouted out the area. A boy, the only other child aboard, intensely watched her from a few seats back on the other side. Their eyes met, and they exchanged waves. He held up a small ball and shook it. "Throw it!" she said. They played until the pilot announced the plane would soon land. John awoke, nudged her, and asked Lirah if she was ready for an adventure. She smiled with a nod. A gentle tap on her right shoulder disturbed her. "Please, give me my ball," he whispered several times. "It is mine now," said Lirah. "Keep your hands off me!" Down his chubby red cheeks tears rolled, so he waddled to the back to wash his face. Lirah slowly followed and then bolted in front of the door, waiting for it to open. Finally, when it did, she swiftly pushed him backwards, which caused him to lacerate his head on the sink. Her malevolent eyes watched blood spill over the floor. *Wonderful!* "My ball," she mouthed, and she skipped back to her seat. She tightly hugged her parents and thanked them for the trip. "Of course, anything for our perfect daughter." Clouds of various shapes and sizes and landscapes relieved Lirah's boredom for the next hour.

CHAPTER 6

SINLESS FLOWER

The plane's wheels brushed along the runway until it made a complete stop. They walked from the airport through the street vendors. The scent of spices pervaded the air, as did singing from nearby children sitting on the ground, clapping along in rhythm. They walked hand in hand, and Lirah saw a woman whose extreme age displayed on her face. *Creepy*, she thought. They eventually reached the Museum of All Wonders, tilting their heads back at the sheer size and extravagance. Lirah noticed what seemed to be an enormous tree atop the roof. They stepped inside, and Lirah immediately wanted to find the flower, but her mother insisted they first explore, because the possibility of visiting again was slim to none. They saw everything from aquariums to fossils to animatronic dinosaur robots. Observing only seemed like an interlude; her mother noticed her vexation. "Mom, may we see the flower now?" "Yes, yes!" John asked a passing janitor where they could find the Sinless Flower, and he pointed them in the right direction. She pulled her mother

along. Violah and John walked as Lirah expeditiously traversed down long flights of stairs and laid eyes upon a colossal flower garden. The garden was indoors but connected to the outside. She observed closely and apprehended that the tree she had conjectured was on the roof was actually growing from the ground; it was just tall enough to be seen over the museum. She read a sign with information about the grand size of the tree, 200 feet high.

Violah questioned the tour guide about where the flower could be found and the reason it was called the Sinless Flower. "Follow me!" she said, and then she explained the power it possessed: to make sinners—wicked children—repent. "Evil children do not exist," Violah remarked. The guide resumed explaining, and in incredulity the three of them shared a smirk and a baffled glance. Violah wondered how a plant could punish young children. It seemed like insignificant, banal prattle to Lirah. She finally laid eyes on the alluring flower and thought it was the most magnificent, odd-looking thing. She reached towards it but was snatched away. "Do not touch it, or you will surely regret it!" "Mind your manners," her father said. "How much is it?" Violah asked. "It is not for sale." "Everything has a price; I am able to pay what you want and more." Gritting her teeth, the guide made it immensely clear it was not sanctioned for purchase.

"Someone is a little uptight," said Violah. Disappointed, Lirah ambled away, with them trailing behind her. "We will look for something in the street-vending area," her father said.

They looked around and noticed that vegetation was much more prevalent than it was back home, and brick-and-mortar structures were scarce. She walked ahead of her parents and spotted the eerie-looking old lady standing behind a sizable red blanket that jewelry was spread over. *Pretty,* she thought. Enthralled by one necklace on the back right-hand corner of the blanket, she hurried to retrieve her father and mother. "Dad, Mom, we can forget the flower. I found something better!" shouted Lirah. "Look, the necklace has the flower inside!" "It does," Violah agreed. "Ma'am, how much for the necklace?" "A price it does not have." "Ugh, this again," Violah uttered. "Free it is, no value monetary can be sought, for this jewelry is not permitted to be bought," the woman said creepily. They asked repeatedly if it was truly free. She assured them it was. Lirah thanked her and grabbed the necklace. "Turn around. I will put it on you," Violah said. "I love it," she exclaimed. They had walked a ways down the street when Violah realized she forgot her purse, and they quickly ran back. She found her purse, but the woman and the blanket were nowhere to be found. Their distraught

appearance drew two vendors to assist them. "Where is that lady with the red blanket who was selling jewelry?" "What are you talking about?" the vendors asked. Violah explained, "The lady who was right there." "There was no one there." Lirah said, "Yes, she was. She gave me this." She dangled it. The vendors trembled and viciously ordered them to leave. "Do not yell at my wife and daughter, or you and I are going to have a serious problem!" Disturbed by their demeanor, along with their loud voices, they left.

CHAPTER 7

THE MAN'S EYES

They arrived at the airport, and once inside the plane and in her seat, Lirah became quite averse to a stranger's looks. She faced front and later realized he was still staring. The man finally closed his eyes; therefore, she thought it was a good time to use the bathroom. As she lathered her hands, a large hand covered her mouth. She became petrified, and a plethora of thoughts raced through her mind. He assured that no harm would come to her and his hand would be removed, as long as she remained quiet. She nodded. He cautiously lowered his hand, and they stared at one another. "What—what are you doing?" "Please, give me your necklace." "No, it is mine!" A passenger opened the door, and she ran out. "What is going on?" shouted the passenger. With his eyes as big as light bulbs, he said, "This is not what you think." An officer approached and cuffed him to the seat. "Listen, let me make something very clear. Stay away from the child; keep your mouth shut," the officer sternly said. "Do you understand me?" He assured him that no

issues would come from him. The passengers took their seats, and everyone settled down as they stared at the man with disgust. The man waited, attached to the seat next to the officer until they landed. Then, the officer took off the cuffs and told him that he never wanted to see his face again.

John placed his hand on his wife's shoulder and held Lirah's hand as they deboarded the plane. When inside the airport lounge, Lirah scowled at her father, demanding he buy her a smoothie. "That is not how you ask, Lirah!" John disciplined her. He told his wife that they would purchase Lirah's favorite. "Do you want anything?" John asked. Violah shook her head and smiled at her husband, completely oblivious to how her daughter just behaved. From a distance, the mysterious man from the plane watched and waited for his chance to approach. When the two returned, Lirah went to the bathroom, hopping all the way there with her legs squished together. Mr. Mystery quickly walked up to them. John whispered, "What are you doing here?" "I mean you no harm. Let me explain. Then I promise I will leave," he said. "Our daughter should not see you; I do not trust you," he told him with his nostrils flaring like a bull. "Would not you want to find out if your daughter was in danger, even if you thought it was not true?" the man inquired. "Our

daughter is fine. Just leave us alone," John said. "I am begging you. You must listen to me. She is going to change," he went on. "Do you not understand what I am saying? Leave me and my family alone. I am warning you!" John demanded. The man walked away with his hands in his pockets. Lirah came back to the table, and John said, "We should go now." They went to the vehicle, and everyone buckled. Violah looked at her husband as she rubbed his hand.

CHAPTER 8

UNDERSTANDING

They finally arrived home from the airport and unloaded their luggage. Violah and John headed to their room and Lirah to hers. Violah said, "I am so tired. I am going to bed. I am glad we were only there a few hours because I do not think that I could stand being in that place a full day." "I know, Honey, you need to sleep in your bed," John said. He went to check on Lirah and told her to brush her teeth. "Lirah, hurry up so you can give your mother a hug before she falls asleep." Lirah looked at him as she froze like a statue. "Lirah, did you hear me?" John asked. She stood stiff as a board. "What is wrong with you?" John looked closely at her eyes and noticed her dilated pupils. "LIRAH! I am serious; answer me," John said. She directed her eyes up towards his face and answered in a calm voice, "Yes, why are you shouting?" "Nothing, go hug your mother," he ordered.

John came in after Lirah and closed the door. "She is acting weird," John told Violah. "Wait, do not tell me you believe that crazy guy," she said. "It is just that her

behavior is different." "So, you both are crazy. She is just being a normal child, and sometimes children misbehave, nothing to be alarmed about," said Violah. "Her eyes look different," said John. "She is fine," she insisted. "You know, you have always babied her. Children need discipline," John said. They agreed to disagree and went to sleep.

One morning, John noticed someone peeking through the stained-glass window, and then a knock at the door followed. "I cannot believe this guy," John mumbled. He answered the door. "What do you want now?" "I told you that I am here to help you and your family. You must get her to give you that necklace," he said. "Keep your voice down," he ordered. "I am sorry," the man said. "I have been patient with you, but you are starting to annoy me. This is the third time I have caught you on our property, the second time you have knocked on our door. Not to mention the first two days when you stood across the street, waiting for us to come outside. Yeah, I saw you, and you should be happy I did not call the police," John whispered. "I need to talk to you and your wife. Then if you still do not want my help, I will leave." "Fine, I will talk to her," he said as he reluctantly agreed. "We will hear you out. Meet us at seven at Leaf Park." "Thank you. By the way, my name is Meo," he said and walked down the stairs to the path and continued onto the cobblestone streets until he was out of sight.

John went up the stairs to break the news to Violah. "She is not going to want to hear this," he mumbled. He decided that it would be better to tell her after she had her morning tea. They sat at the nook, eating. He tapped his fingers. "What is wrong?" she asked. "We need to talk," he replied. "Oh no, I hope it is nothing serious." "Do you remember that guy from the plane?" "Yes," she answered. "He has been coming here since that day." "Are you joking? Why did you not tell me that stalker freak was coming to our home? Do you mean to tell me this has been going on for over a week, and you have not said anything to me?" she said as she ran her fingers through her hair. "I was trying to avoid this kind of conversation right here," he told her. She let out a sigh as she rubbed his arm. "What does he want?" she asked. John explained what Meo said. "This is too much," Violah said. "I think we should just hear him out," John said. "What time do we need to be there?" "Seven," he answered.

The time was approaching quickly for them to meet Meo. They fixed Lirah a meal and told her to eat and then play a game until they returned. As they drove to the park, Violah was inquisitive about the man. They arrived and saw him standing next to a large oak tree.

They exited their vehicle and slowly trailed towards him. Eyebrows down, John demanded answers. "You must get her to take it off, or she is going to die!" "You sure do have a way of starting conversations," John said, "You are talking about the necklace, right?" he asked. "Difficult as this may be to hear, it is the truth." He continued, telling them that his family and him were members of a secret society that saved nefarious children from an ocean grave. "I do not want to say this, but your child is evil, a murderer." "How do you have the audacity to utter something so preposterous?" John began to lose his temper. "The blue ring around the necklace was green, which indicated the wearer has intentionally taken life," he explained. "Our society is called Matemkon, which means forgiveness and grace". He pulled out a book from his bag that elaborated the necklaces' purpose, what each color denoted, and the punishments of each sin. "Children are sinners, too. Some people are just born evil." "This is a bunch of drivel. We are leaving—you are crazy!" Violah said. They turned to leave and took a few steps before Meo said, "Her necklace was purple when you bought it, then green, then blue, and now it should be white, I presume, and the fairy's hands moved." Hearing the truth stopped them in their tracks. "How did you know that?" they asked in unison. Violah said,

"I thought it was a mood necklace, like a mood ring, new technology or something, and that was how I thought the fairy's arms were able to move." Meo said, "The arms are like the hands of a clock, and she had exactly twelve days from the time she first put it on. The changes have already begun, and it will become worse." John looked at Violah. "This seems unreal," John said to Meo. "Each day you will notice differenc-es in her personality and behavior."

They were shocked. "What do we...how do we save our daughter?" "She must willingly give you the necklace. Not saying it will not be difficult." "Why can we not just take it?" she asked. "Because trust is the first step to righteousness, and that would be stealing," Meo answered. "A spirit follows and controls events that surround the wearer to prevent it from being re-moved—coincidences, you can say. Once the twelve days are up, her soul will be trapped within the neck-lace," he told them. "This seems impossible," Violah uttered. "Her caged soul will be forced to watch as the Tehmahgrun overtakes her. The creature is so hideous to humans that the mere sight has killed or caused insanity." "What do you mean exactly?" John asked. "The Tehmahgrun will come out of her body, and we need to stop it from happening." They still looked at Meo in opposition. "Please, trust me. If it is true, you

would have saved her life. If not, she just loses a neck-lace—an object," Meo urged. "We believe you, as crazy as it sounds," John said. "Once you get her to give you the necklace, Violah, bring it to Whistleleaf Beach, be-hind the rocks. I will meet you there," said Meo. "How did you know my name?" They sped home.

They pondered the information as they sat in the driveway. "There is no way that this could possibly happen, could it?" Violah asked. She placed her head on the dashboard. Violah asked, "Why our daughter?" "We need to deal with this. Meo did know things that he should not have, but I just do not know." They went inside, only to find that Lirah was out of sight. "Lirah, Lirah," she called out. "Where is she?" A tap on her back startled Violah. They turned around to Lirah's blank stare. Lirah ran quickly up the stairs. "What was that about?" John asked. Violah went to make dinner, and John told her to take a rest and that he would cook instead. She went into the living room and drifted off to sleep, and a dream haunted her mind. In the dream she saw light in the sky over a furious ocean. She watched a tornado descend from the sky into the depths of the ocean, into a dark place, as dark as obsidian. Feelings of turmoil, sadness, and absolute fear filled her heart like a deluge. A face of a horrifying creature rushed her as the wind from the force of the creature pushed

her into a large cage and on her back and afflicted her with great pain. Violah tried to move when she heard a soft voice. She rolled over, and there was a small figure clenching the bars. Taking a closer look, she could see that it was her daughter. "Lirah!" she called out. "Save me," she said weakly. She looked drained and in pain, like she had been beaten and dragged through a fire. Violah's eyes became as big as marbles as Lirah began to cough uncontrollably, until the Sinless Flower fell onto the stone floor from out of her chest as if her chest were made of water. Violah woke up screaming to John holding down her arms. "Honey, calm down!" he said. "I think Meo is right. I had a dream, only it was not. It was so real," she told him. She began to tell him what she saw. John made an eleven between his eyebrows. He grabbed her shoulders and told her he believed her.

Day 11

After shopping they returned, and their vehicle's lights on the house exposed the curtains partially hanging from the window. Their mouths dropped as they pushed open the front door. Their house was in shambles while Lirah sat with her legs crossed in the middle of the floor, vigorously scratching into her mirror with her nails what looked to be letters, yet there was no blood. "Lirah, Lirah, LIRAH!" John shouted. "What are

you...what did you do?" "Not this again," John said to himself. Lirah looked around the room. Violah told her to give her the necklace, because she thought it was pretty and did not want her to lose it. "No, take it, and I will kill you!" As Violah reached for her shoulder, Lirah squeezed her hand until she yelled. Her mother's agonizing voice snapped her out of the trance. "Why is everything messed up?" Lirah asked. "Come in the kitchen; I will make you a smoothie," Violah said to keep her unaware of her discomfort and keep her calm. John asked for the necklace, to get a better look and so he could have one made for her mother to wear for her birthday party. Her breath slowed, and her eyes blinked like waking from sleep. As she reached for the necklace, the ceiling lights exploded. Tiny cuts bled from his face. They ran out of the violently shaking house before it partially collapsed. The three of them hopped into the van, and he wiped the blood from his cheek. John drove to the beach, frantically running red lights, dodging anything in their path. Beats of their hearts reverberated in their chests. "Honey, please give me the necklace," Violah begged. Lightning began to repeatedly strike the ocean and the sand. The beach-goers went on about mingling, eating, and drinking their piña coladas, unable to see what was occurring. By the time they arrived at the spot, Lirah's eyes were

wide open and dilated, and her body was hard as a brick. "Just carry her!" Violah screamed.

They stumbled along the coast, calling out for Meo. As her pupils turned white, they knew it was too late. She became heavier as he carried her, almost to the point that he was unable to lift her. Her body hit the sand. "What is going on?" Violah asked. "She is so heavy. It feels like she weighs two hundred pounds," he said. "Help me!" he shouted. They each took one of her arms to drag her across the sand but only traversed a few meters before they were exhausted. "I cannot pull her anymore. She is too heavy and becoming heavier," she said. "Where is he?" asked John. John turned around and slammed into Meo. He grabbed him by the shirt. "Where were you?" "I came here as fast I could, no car." Meo told them to step back. "That is not her anymore." "Save her!" Violah begged. "It is too late!" said Meo. The necklace illuminated the beach while her soul came out of her body, as if being sucked into the necklace like thousands of specks of dust wisped into a portal. Unadulterated devastation and fear became part of them as her fingernails hit the sand and her face began to appear deformed. Two long, jagged nailed hands ripped out of the top of her head, pulling it apart into two halves. Four wings that faced each direction fluttered, shredding her body into dozens of

pieces. The sharp teeth of the mouths of the wings vigorously chomped. John and Violah's feet were covered in blood. It had horns on its knees on each of its seven legs, fur like a bear on its back, and two feet of an iguana on each leg—one facing north and one south facing. The Tehmahgrun stepped out of her mutilated corpse, towering over them. They held one another, trying to grab some air.

The old lady appeared, and they recognized her—the woman who gave Lirah the necklace. The wave of her hand over their eyes extracted their fright. They came to and questioned the reason for her presence and why this was happening. "What are you? Who are you?" John asked. "I am that who has no name," she answered. She told them that their daughter had massacred many people with no contrition. She placed one palm on each of their heads to expose Lirah's heinous behavior. Instantly, they finally understood the veracious nature of their daughter; they were appalled by how deluded they had been for the past few years. They saw that she sliced Jimmy's Achilles tendon with a broken piece of glass, deliberately surprised her aunt and uncle, causing them to stumble down the stairs, and the many other deaths. The woman removed her hands. At that moment, they experienced betrayal to the fullest extent by their daughter's travesty of sweetness. Lirah was just a child to them,

their baby, their daughter. They wondered why their child and what they did wrong. The woman proclaimed they were the cause of Lirah's behavior and disposition because of their dysfunctional parenting. Their love was the pretext for the consistent showering of gifts and praise and the meagerness of instilling respect, which were indicative of their endearment, though not what she needed to mature into a kind individual. "Do you believe in God?" the woman asked. "We thought that was man-made. We have everything beyond our dreams of avarice: cars, a house, family, friends, and all the money we could possibly desire. We had no reason to look for God," Violah said. "You are filled with so much anger," the woman said. "He took my father. I prayed, we prayed every day, and he still took him," she said as her sobbing became more intense. "Your pain is understood but irrelevant. **Losing someone does not negate God's existence.** Parents who are not believers may have children who follow suit. To show the severity of sin, her soul will be tortured for seven years and imprisoned in the ocean." With her voice trembling with remorse, she shrieked out, "I believe." "We do, we see that we were wrong; God, please help us!" John bellowed out. "Quite ironic that people cry God when in trouble but blaspheme when all is well," she said with a wry smile. "We will see how honest you were. You are saying this now,

but if this did not happen, you would never think about God." Violah bowed her head.

She saw that they wanted forgiveness, so she was willing to make them a deal. She informed them that Lirah would remain in the Tehmahgrun dimension until Judgment Day unless one of them paid for their sins that had led Lirah astray by taking Lirah's place for six dimension-years. Only then would Lirah's soul be released to a peaceful holding place after one year of torture. She asked why she needed to be tortured at all. "Justice must be served," she replied. Their knees struck the beach, and John banged his fists on the sand. A puddle formed beneath their eyes. "You say our daughter is evil, but look what just came out of her," John said. "You humans do not regard punishment to be a reasonable ramification for egregious conduct, always making justifications for your actions. The Tehmahgrun are not evil; they do their duty, as police do theirs," the woman explained. They argued back and forth about who would take the sentence. Violah said that she should, because of her coddling of Lirah and overriding of John's authority when he was not home. The decision displeased him, but he finally relented. She stood and let go of her husband's hand. "I will take the six years for our daughter." "The decision will be final. Are you certain?" the woman asked. She looked into his eyes, they told one another they loved

each other, and she apologized for what she had done. "This is as much my fault as it is yours," John sobbed while touching the soft skin of her cheek. She touched Violah's head, and she collapsed. With her head on his lap, he yelled her name in an attempt to wake her, to no avail. The woman told John that he would see his wife again and that patience was a precious commodity. Then, she vanished.

With sand beneath his feet and water up to his knees, he felt the waves brush against his body, back and forth. A hand touched his shoulder, "I am so, so sorry this happened to you," Meo said. John's breath moved his chest up and down, and his eyes could not close. "We tried for days to get her to give us the necklace. I did so much research in every book I could get my hands on. Nothing told us how to help, and because of my stubbornness I did not listen to you. Now my daughter and wife are gone." His eyes reflected the pinkish-purple hue of the sky. His head shook from side to side ever so slightly. John held his head with his elbow supported by his knees, so confused because he could not fathom how a necklace could create such turmoil. Meo assured him that none of what occurred was because of the necklace. He explained that the Sinless Flower was sent to the earth to reveal to parents that being a parent was paramount.

Everyone began life in complete ignorance, and parents have authority to give their offspring the opportunity to know God. Parents or those playing that role, should be the first ones to introduce God to their children. "Each flower produced three necklaces, and the watchers positioned them to be taken by children who perpetrate unquestionable sins." "I am so sorry I did not follow you, God," John said quietly. " Do not keep this a secret," Meo said. "Spread the word."

CHAPTER 9

SLEEP AND WAIT

We stumble upon John reading the good book to Violah. The silence was nearly unbearable to him. The only thing allowing him to hold on was his rekindled faith and the hankering that she would return to him. He knew she did right by their daughter. His mindset, his morals, and his look on life were completely transformed; God was his new cynosure.

He gazed at his wife's frozen face as she lay in a hospital bed—the bed where she would remain for five consecutive months more. To others, she seemed to only be in a coma. He kissed Violah's forehead as he whispered, "I love you so much. I am waiting." He stroked his wife's hair while he deeply stared, as if he could see her soul. The window flung open, and her flowing hair danced against the floor. Startled, he turned. It was nothing but the wind, he realized, as red and yellow leaves beyond the lake drew his admiration near, while the autumn wind carried them to the ground. "Thank you, God," he said. Fresh, brisk air filled his lungs. The nearly bare trees made him reminisce about walks in

the park with his family. John continued to return to the hospital every day, and as time went on, he worshipped by placing his head on the floor, repenting and saying prayers of appreciation.

One day, John headed to the hospital for his daily ritual. As he drove, his excitement grew, for he knew that day would be what he had been waiting for all of those months. He arrived and parked his car. John opened the door and ran to the hospital and up the stairs to his wife's room. He gasped for air as the doors opened. Approaching her bedside, he slowly inhaled and exhaled. He grabbed a seat to wait out the anticipation. His head lay sideways with his arms stretched over her legs. After a while, her fingers caressed his curls, and he turned his head towards her. "You are awake," he stuttered. John and Violah shared an embrace; they could not let each other go. "It is over now, but we must both believe. I know you did all those years back. Now I do as well. I am sorry for not believing you and forcing you to choose me over God," she said as she sniffled. "One more thing, we must warn others how severe sin is and that God is truly forgiving. One day we will see our little girl again," John said as he held his wife. "I am so grateful that God gave me a second chance," said Violah. She finally truly understood His love and that they must trust in Him. He

is the only way. They spent the rest of the day in the word and embracing their newfound love for God and one another.

CHAPTER 10

FIFTY YEARS

Fifty years in the future, at a nursing home, a group of four young adults sat in a gazebo, listening to a riveting story. When the story ended, they could not wrap their minds around what they just heard and became a little uncomfortable. "Well, we should go," said Trent. "Have a good day," they all said. The elderly woman grabbed one of the young ladies, Jisal, by the hand and said, "Remember that God is everything, and you are nothing without him. Repent for your sins, and please, I beg you, do not make the same mistakes we did." Jisal glanced at the couple and said, "Sure, Mrs. Imra, see you next time."

AFTERWORD

You see, earthly wealth is revered, but reluctance is shown towards seeking godly wealth. True wealth can only be obtained through God. True faith is real wealth, which will be received in heaven for those who on earth were true believers and, above all, placed God first. Like many others, Lirah's parents were guilty of not desiring the grace of God over material wealth. Look what happened to them. Luckily, they learned their lesson. It is never too late to learn yours.